The Book that Jack made

Paul and Emma Rogers

THE BODLEY HEAD
LONDON

This is the page that should be at the back.
If you're wondering what happened, you'd better ask Jack.

This is the page where he wrote out a song,
But crossed it all out 'cos he kept going wrong.

This is the page, all crumpled and creased,
That his brother screwed up, the horrible beast.

There was once a boy called Jack

me

who lived with his dad

and his baby brother.

They had no money.
His dad said, 'we
haven't got a bean.
You must go to town
and sell the cow.'

So off Jack went.

Next comes the page where he spilled all the glue
And never could open it (neither will you!)

This is a picture of Jack leaving town.
(A pity he put it in upside down.)

Jack swapped the cow for a bag of
beans. Everyone said they were magic.

This is a picture of Dad in a rage
But the baby threw breakfast all over the page.

But his dad didn't believe it.

'Stupid boy!

what use are these?'

and he threw the beans away.

one bean grew AND grew

and grew!

Now they had **millions** of beans.

This is the page where he painted the sky
And then turned it over before it was dry.

They weren't hungry anymore.

They had boiled beans

fried beans

baked beans
(without the toast)

bean pie

bean soup

bean stew

bean salad

Next comes the page that got nibbled by mice
And littered with mouse droppings (not very nice).

'Not beans again! I'm fed up with beans!' said Jack.

This is the page, all blurry and stained,
That he left outside when it rained and rained.

'I think I'll go up
and see what's at
the top.'

A GIANT!

This is the one that was too big to fit,
So he folded and cut it (which spoiled it a bit).

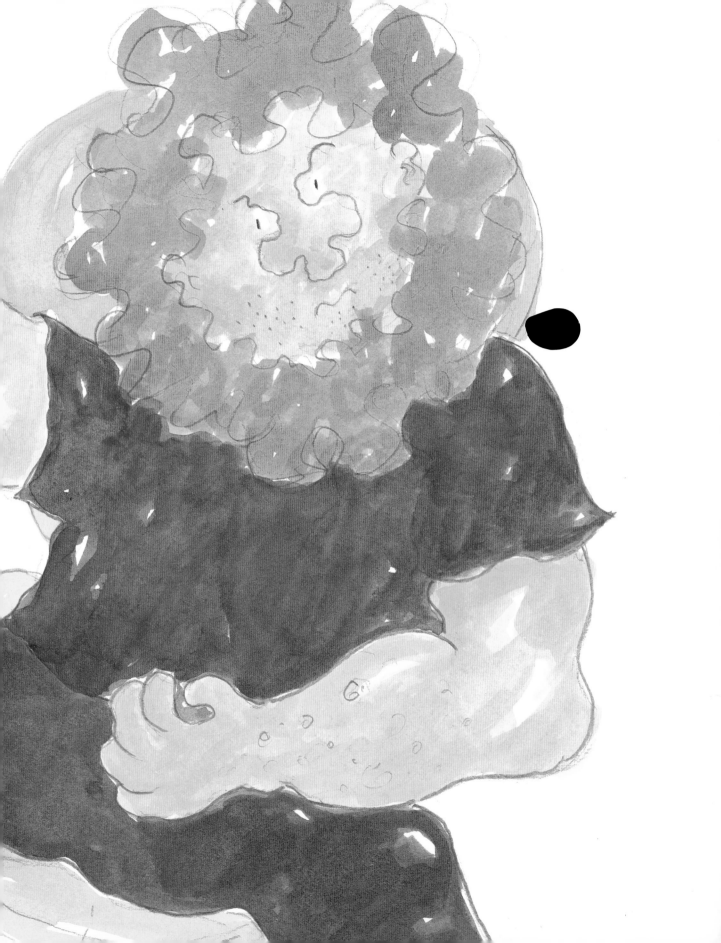

He spotted JACK
and chased him.

This is a picture he kept trying to do,
But he rubbed it so hard that he went right through.

This is the page that was ever so neat
Till a cat walked across it with mud on its feet.

'Fee Fi Fo Fum

You'll soon wish
you hadn't come!'

chop Chop Chop

The giant came
tumbling down.
BOOM!

That's the end
of him.

Next comes the page that the baby tore out.
(I have no idea what that was about.)

out it all

ippee!'

ce that's all there seems to be,
better go back to the start to see
nd of the book that Jack made.

clever old Jack!

that's me →

I bet you couldn't make
one like this!